The SPUR BOOK of WEATHER LORE

Also in the
SPURBOOK VENTURE GUIDE
SERIES . . .

By Brown and Hunter

Map and Compass
Basic Sailing
Snorkelling
Outdoor First Aid
Knots, Bends and Hitches (2nd Ed.)
Camping
Starting to Ski

In Preparation:

Small Boat Handling (1977)
Fitness for the Family (1977)
Survival and Rescue (1976)
Chart and Compass by Ted Broadhurst
Back Packing by Robin Adshead (1977)
Hill-Trekking by Peter Lumley (1977)
Dinghy Cruising by Margaret Dye (1977)

SPUR FOOTPATH GUIDES
include . . .

Walks Along the South Downs Way (2nd edn.)
Walks in South Essex
Walks West of London
Walks in the New Forest
Chiltern Round Walks
Walks in Hertfordshire
Midland Walks
Walks in the Surrey Hills (3rd Ed.)
Walks in the Hills of Kent
Walks in Berkshire
Walks in the Cotswolds
Walks in Oxfordshire
Walks in Dorset

The SPUR BOOK of WEATHER LORE

by
Terry Brown and Rob Hunter

SPURBOOKS LIMITED

Published 1976 by
Spurbooks Ltd.
6 Parade Court
Bourne End
Bucks

The authors and publishers would like to thank the staff of the Meteorological Office, Bracknell, Berkshire, for their advice and assistance in the preparation of this book.

ISBN 0 904978 21 4

Printed by Maund & Irvine, Ltd., Tring, Herts.

LIST OF CONTENTS

INTRODUCTION

ABOUT THIS SERIES

Venture guides are designed and written for people who enjoy outdoor activities in all weathers. They aim to provide such people with a range of basic information and knowledge on which to ground their activities, in order that their activities can be both safer and more fun.

Venture Guides therefore cover such outdoor Skills as Knot Tying, Map and Compass Work, Camping, Sailing and Snorkelling, First Aid, and now Weather Lore. Further titles will cover Survival and Rescue and Physical Fitness, the whole series providing an essential library for the outdoor man.

ABOUT THIS BOOK

Any outdoor activity, from an Everest expedition to the vicarage fête, is influenced by the weather. In the United Kingdom the weather is a constant source of interest and conversation, even to people whose idea of recreation is bar-billiards, because the weather in the U.K., whatever else it is, is variable. It has been wryly commented that while some countries have a climate, Britain just has lots of weather.

Britain is a largely urban society, where people are protected by central heating, or car heaters, from the worst effects of winter, and when, therefore, the British take up outdoor sports and pastimes, like climbing, sailing, rambling, or camping, they encounter weather as never before, and not infrequently the experience comes as a great shock.

This book is not designed to teach even elementary meteorology—if there can be such a thing.

This book introduces the reader to the elements of weather, to those winds, currents, clouds, temperatures and atmospheres that make up our 'weather', and shows how the ordinary outdoor enthusiast can learn about the weather, and write weather information into his outdoor activity plans.

It is a regrettable fact that while most outdoor people love making lists, and go to great lengths to equip themselves with *'Food', 'Clothing', 'Maps'* etc. there is rarely a heading that reads *'Weather'*. And yet the weather is the one factor that affects all the rest. So if we can achieve no more in this book, than to have outdoor people adding *'Weather'* to the list of headings on their check-list we will feel this book is well worth while.

STRATOSPHERE
TROPOPAUSE
HIGHEST
MOUNTAINS
TROPOSPHERE
SEA LEVEL
THE ATMOSPHERE

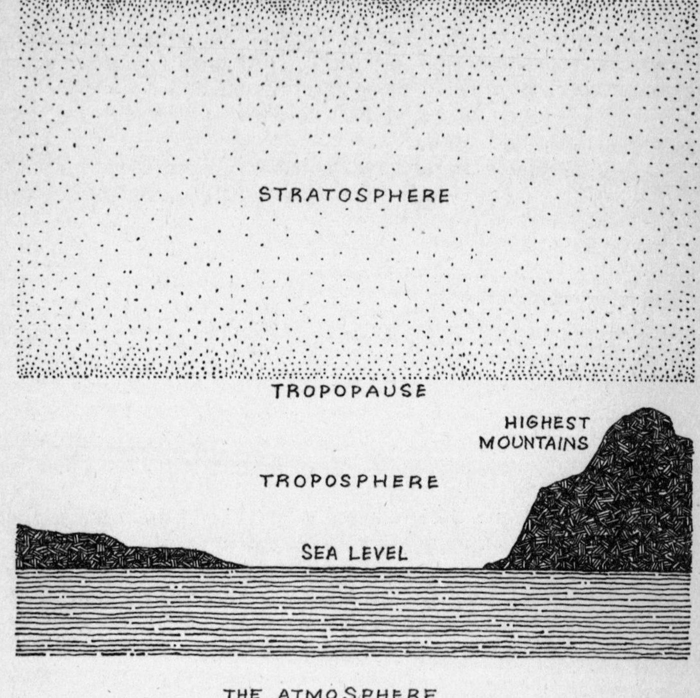

Fig. 1.

Chapter 1

THE ELEMENTS OF WEATHER

The 'weather' is, as we all know, a very variable thing, which can change several times a day. Various elements—and we use the word in its colloquial sense—go to make up this weather brew, notably atmosphere, pressure, wind, humidity, temperature, seasonal variations, and local conditions. There is never anything static about the weather, but there are some general points which hold good most of the time and need to be known. Let us first, however, look at these elements.

ATMOSPHERE

The world is wrapped in a big envelope of breathable air, called the atmosphere. The atmosphere extends for about 100 miles above the surface of the earth and is divided into various layers, (Fig. 1).

The first of these layers is the Troposphere, which goes up to about 5 miles, and this is followed by the Tropopause, while above this again is the Stratosphere. The weather, as it affects us, is usually found in the Troposphere.

It is sufficient to know that the earth is cocooned in air. This atmosphere is subjected to various forces, the chief of which is pressure, caused by the gravitational pull of the earth.

PRESSURE

At sea-level the pressure of the atmosphere—that is the weight of the air on the earth, is about 14lbs per sq. inch. Pressure comes from all sides, and nobody really notices it, but pressure is very significant in meteorology and weather lore. As a *general* rule, falling pressure indicates the approach of bad weather, while rising pressure indicates good weather. But please note the 'general'. There are few absolutes in weather.

Pressure is measured in *bars*—and the instrument which measures pressure is now therefore called a barometer. You can buy proper aneroid barometers, for use at home, for less than £20, and quite adequate portable ones for about £3. (Fig. 2).

Barometers should be kept in a cool spot with steady temperatures. The hall is much better than the kitchen. In meteorological circles the bar is divided into millibars (mb.) and the normal air pressure at *sea-level* is 1013 millibars; but, as we should note, pressure varies, and rises and falls in the pressure, from the 1000mb. mark, are good pointers to the weather. The limits of pressure usually lie between 950mb. and 1050mb.

Fig. 2.

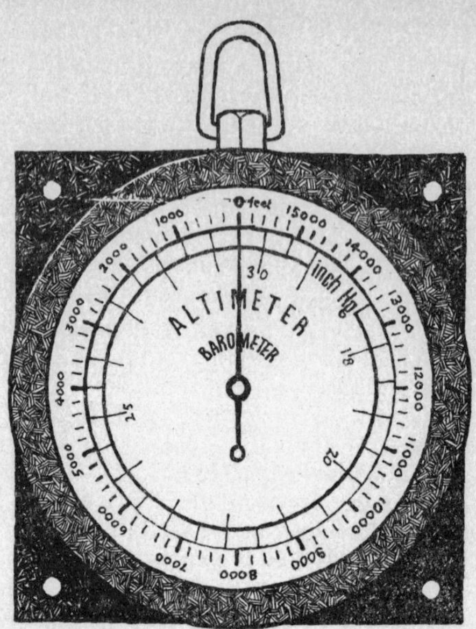

A HANDY POCKET BAROMETER

Remember that this pressure is *sea-level* pressure. As you rise up in an aeroplane or while climbing, for example, the pressure will drop. So you need to adjust for height by getting the correct pressure setting for your area by phoning the local Met. Office. Official weather forecasts give barometric pressure in millibars, adjusted for sea-level. Pressure falls about 1 mb every 30 feet, so if you are on top of a 3000 ft. mountain, a pressure of 900mb. on your pocket barometer indicates quite normal weather. So don't forget the height. Most household barometers are calibrated in inches; 29.9 inches is the same as 1013mb. and is normal pressure. So, when pressure on your household barometer rises into the 30s or falls to about 27, you can look for changes in the weather.

On a weather map, points of equal pressure are joined up by lines called *isobars.* Isobars join points of equal pressure in the same way as contour lines join points of equal height. We shall return to this later, but just read this again, before we go on to the next point.

TEMPERATURE

Temperature is measured with a thermometer, and in weather lore, the important temperature is the 'true air temperature', taken in the *shade*. Sometimes this temperature is recorded on a device called a thermograph, which can often be seen functioning in museums and some public buildings. These bi-metallic devices consist of a central core of two metals welded together. Temperature changes cause these metals to expand or contract at different rates, and the result is recorded on a paper chart moving on a revolving drum. A clinical thermometer, the sort you stick in your mouth, will not do to record air temperatures, but expanding metal thermometers are available from Stationers or Car Equipment shops, and you can obtain decent outdoor thermometers from about £1.50 from most outdoor equipment shops.

Temperature is now expressed in Centigrade (or Celsius) which is a scale based on the melting and boiling points of water. These are 0°C and 100°C respectively.

The other scale still in common use is the Fahrenheit scale. In this the same base is used, but the freezing point is 32°F and the boiling point 212°F. Many people in the U.K. are more familiar with the Fahrenheit scale than with the centigrade scale. The Fahrenheit degree is about half the centigrade scale, but for an accurate conversion you can use the following formula:

Centigrade temperature x 2 = X — 1/10 = X + 32 = Temp. °F.

So:

20°C x 2 = 40° — 4 = 36 + 32 = 68°F.

So:

20°C = 68°F.

Complicated, isn't it? A simple rule to remember is that 16°C = 61°F and you can work from there.

For the outdoor man, frost and chill on the one hand and high temperatures on the other, need to be reckoned with. Anything below 1°C or 34°F and above 25°C or 75°F need to be taken into account in your expedition plans.

Next, and related to temperature, is the third element, humidity.

HUMIDITY

The atmosphere always contains a certain amount of water vapour, and when this vapour condenses we get different types of weather; especially dew, fog, rain, snow, or the most obvious example, clouds.

The air can only hold just so much water vapour in any form, and when this maximum point is reached the air is said to be saturated. Warm air can hold more vapour than cold air, and it is when warm air is saturated that outdoor people can get heatstroke. The air is too full of water vapour to hold any more, and sweat cannot evaporate from the skin.

Relative humidity is expressed in percentages, so we say that the temperature is so much, say 75°F with 80% humidity, which would be sticky. If the humidity is low, we can have crisp, dry, invigorating air, if the temperature is not high. If the humidity is high, and the temperature high also, we have sultry or muggy weather.

As the temperature falls, air cools, and it can cool until condensation results. This point, the point at which condensation occurs, is called the *dew point.*

Remember that cold air holds less water than warm air and that cold air tends to sink, for these facts are relevant to a lot of weather phenomena.

If there is more vapour than the air can hold, the surplus condenses into clouds, dew etc. If the air currents are strong, the surplus will be held in suspension, but if they are weak, the surplus falls as rain, snow, or dew.

WIND

The next weather ingredient is wind—which can be described most simply as air in a hurry.

If we hark back to pressure, we can note first that wind is usually heading from where pressure is high to where pressure is low. It is trying to fill up the difference. Owing to the rotation of the earth, air currents or winds are usually steered off their direct course, thereby producing those whorls on the weather maps which show wind direction.

Wind is described in two ways; speed and direction.

The speed can be expressed in miles per hour, knots (sea miles per hour) or the graduations of the Beaufort Scale (Fig. 3), a system largely employed at sea. Wind force is measured with an instrument called an anenometer.

Wind direction refers to the direction the wind is coming *FROM,* not going to. So that a wind blowing from Cornwall to Yorkshire is a South-Westerly, not a North-Easterly.

Many parts of the world have 'prevailing winds', that is, the wind blows most often from the same direction. This can be noticed by the effect the prevailing wind has on trees—as in

BEAUFORT WIND SCALE

Beaufort Number	Limits of Wiod Speed in Knots	Descriptive Terms	Sea Criterion	Land Conditions
0	Less than 1	Calm	Like a mirror.	Smoke rises vertically.
1	1–3	Light air	Ripples but without foam crests.	Flags flap slightly.
2	4–6	Light breeze	Small wavelets with unbroken crests.	Leaves rustle; wind felt on face.
3	7–10	Gentle breeze	Large wavelets, with perhaps scattered white horses.	Leaves in motion; flags flap.
4	11–16	Moderate breeze	Small waves; frequent white horses.	Dust rises; branches sway.
5	17–21	Fresh breeze	Moderate waves, more pronounced; many white horses; perhaps some spray.	Small trees sway.
6	22–27	Strong breeze	Large waves forming; extensive white foam crests; likelihood of spray.	Telephone lines whistle; umbrellas hard to hold.
7	28–33	Near gale	Sea heaps up with white foam blown in streaks along direction of wind.	Trees sway; hard to walk.
8	34–40	Gale	Moderately high waves; foam blown in definite streaks along direction of wind.	Twigs fall; cars buffeted.
9	41–47	Strong gale	High waves; crests tumble and roll.	Twigs fall; cars buffetted.
10	48–55	Storm	Very high waves; heavy tumbling waves; poor visibility.	Trees fall.
11	56–63	Violent storm	Exceptionally high waves. Sea completely covered with long white of foam lying along direction of wind. Wave crests blown into froth. Poor visibility.	Check Insurance.
12	64+	Hurricane	Air filled with foam and spray. Very poor visibility.	Pray.

Fig. 3.

Cornwall for example, where many trees lean to the north-east, bent as they grow by the prevailing south-westerly winds.

Wind temperatures vary according to their direction, the time of year, and the surface they pass over. In winter winds coming directly from the East, across Europe, will be colder than the North-Easterlies or Northerlies which pick up some warmth (or lose some chill) crossing the sea.(Fig. 4).

In winter also, in the U.K., south and westerly winds are wet and (relatively) warm, for they pick up moisture crossing the Atlantic, and the sea in winter tends to be warmer than the land. Because these winds are warmer they can hold more moisture. and bring cloudy weather and prolonged periods of rain. Conversely, as we have noted, northern and easterly winds in winter tend to be dry and very cold. In summer, the easterly winds can be warmer, for in summer the land warms up more quickly than the sea, and the winds pick up heat while blowing over it. Remember a northerly wind has a sea passage and is neither as dry in summer nor as cold in winter as an easterly one, (Fig. 4) but this warming of the arctic air can trigger off snow falls.

Winds are very variable, and can blow at different speeds and directions according to height. High altitude winds can be quite different from winds at sea level.

RADIATION

Radiation, especially from the sun, has a great effect on the weather. The sun's radiation action on water vapour or other ingredients in the air, produces clouds, creates warm currents, and begins the convection process which leads to the rainfall cycle. Radiation from the sun provides the energy to drive the weather system.

LOCAL VARIATIONS AND CONDITIONS

There are, of course, many other smaller ingredients in the weather mix, most notably the effect of local geography, on an overall weather pattern. You must, as an outdoor man or woman, find out all you can about local weather conditions. Ask for information from everyone you meet, and by 'local' we mean where you go wandering at weekends as well as where you live.

However, these six are the main components of the weather, and if you begin your study of weather lore by appreciating that it all relates back to these basic factors, then you will have made a good start.

ARCTIC MARITIME
POLAR MARITIME
POLAR MARITIME
POLAR CONTINENTAL
TROPICAL MARITIME
TROPICAL CONTINENTAL

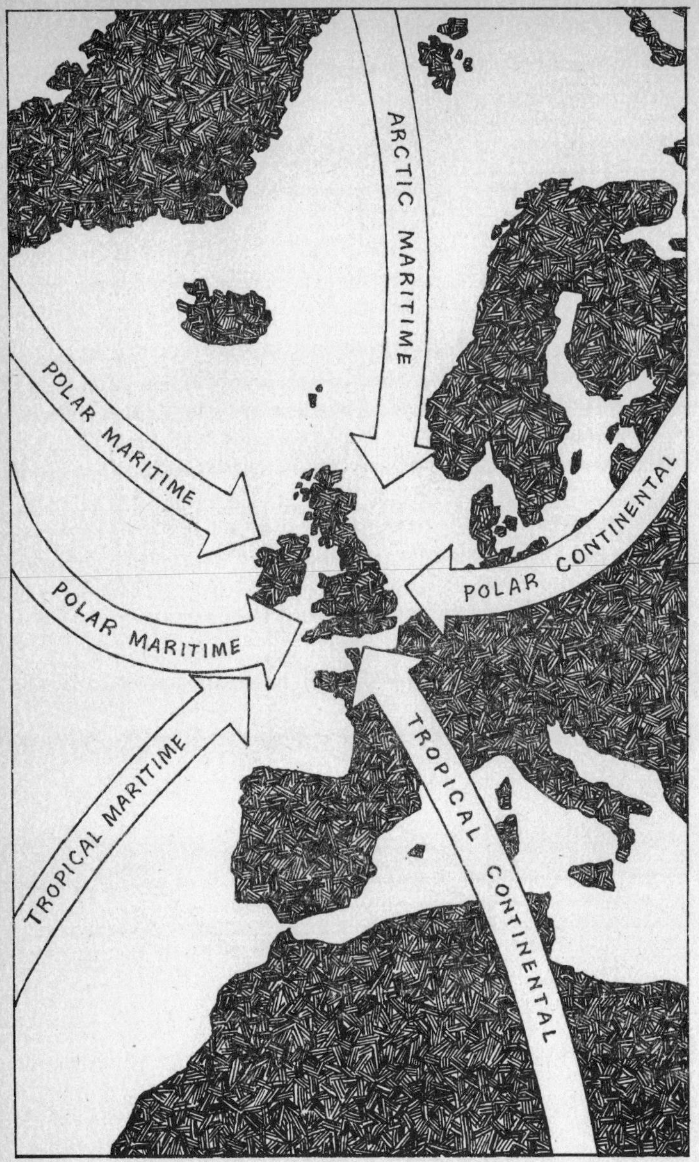

Fig. 4.

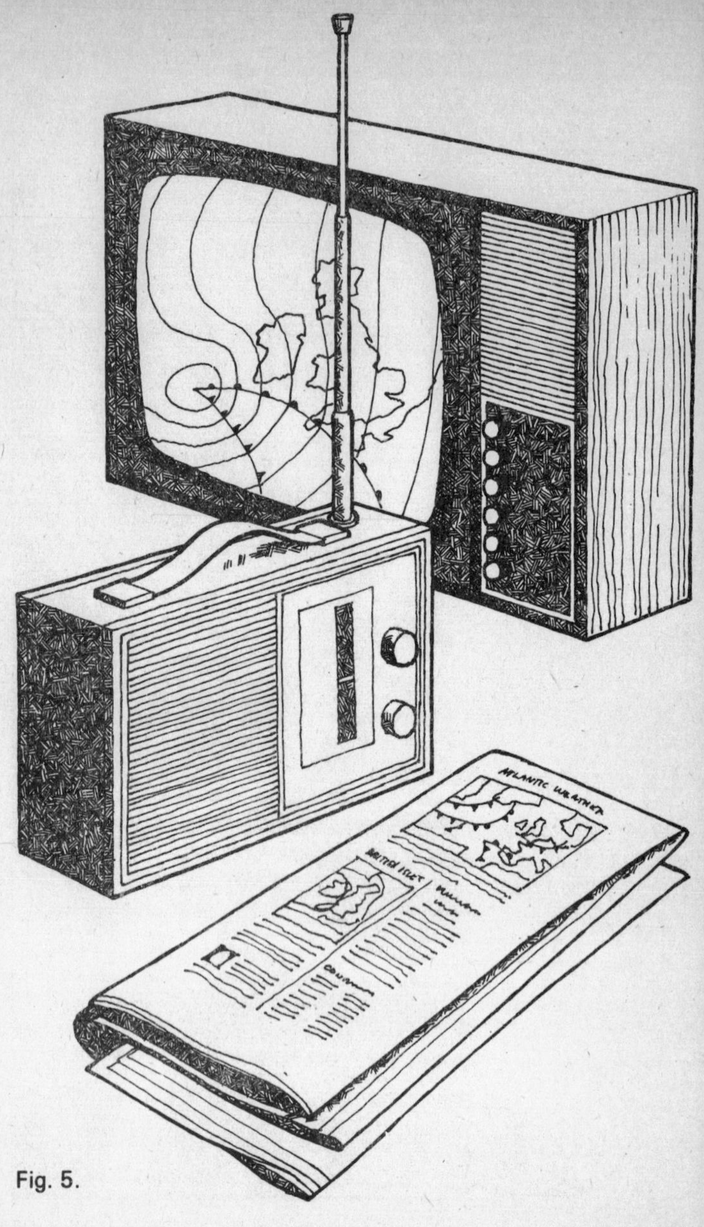

Fig. 5.

Chapter 2

WEATHER FORECASTS

It is not really necessary for the outdoor man or woman to have any knowledge of weather lore at all. You can get all the information you need, and more than you could probably understand, from weather forecasts published in the National or local Press, or broadcast on the radio, or T.V.

FORECAST SOURCES

THE PRESS: Most newspapers publish weather forecasts of varying coverage and use. Some show maps of the U.K. or Europe, and give lots of information. However, you must remember that newspaper information, because it has to be collected, printed, and distributed, is probably at least 12 to 24 hours out of date; and weather conditions can change rapidly. 'The Times' forecast is among the best of the daily Press forecasts, and 'The Guardian' Saturday forecast is excellent. Most 'quality' newspapers have good forecasts.

TELEVISION: The television forecasts, especially the 'Late Night' ones on BBC 1, which give forecasts for three days ahead, can be most useful. They usually show isobars, describe incoming weather, and give predictions on the weather to be encountered at sea or on high ground.

These forecasts are presented on all T.V. channels, usually close to News time. See the Radio or T.V. Times for details.

RADIO FORECASTS (INLAND): These are on Radio 4 and give outlook forecasts for up to two days ahead. They usually concern inland areas, but this can be useful as well to coastal yachtsmen. There is a comprehensive 4 minute forecast for land and sea areas on Radio 3 (464m) medium wave, at 6.55 a.m. on weekdays and 7.55 a.m. on Saturdays and Sundays but check the Radio Times as these times are subject to change.

Radio 4 forecasts include regional reports, and details can be found in the Radio Times.

LOCAL RADIO FORECASTS: The development of local radio stations has been a boon to outdoor people. These stations provide up to the minute local forecasts, often obtained from local as well as national sources, and they take into account local conditions, and up date the information with each broadcast.

See the Radio Times for details of local station broadcasts. Radio Solent, Radio Medway, Radio Cleveland and Radio Newcastle in particular give excellent local forecasts.

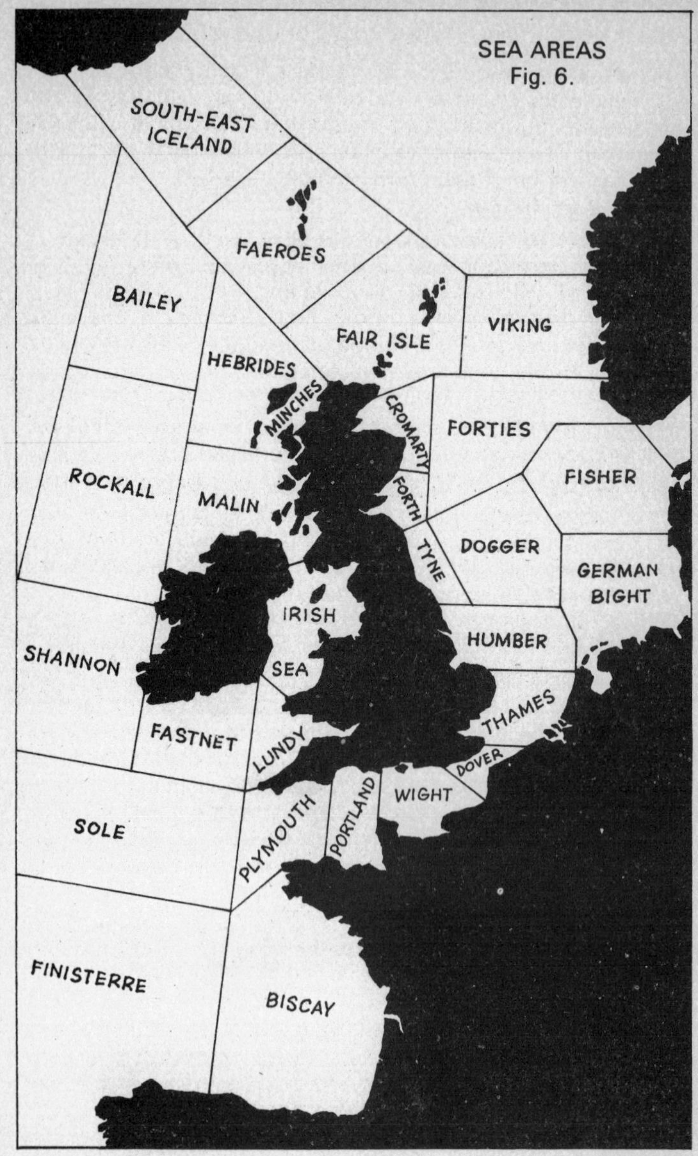
SEA AREAS
Fig. 6.
SOUTH-EAST ICELAND
FAEROES
BAILEY
FAIR ISLE
VIKING
HEBRIDES
MINCHES
CROMARTY
FORTIES
FISHER
ROCKALL
MALIN
FORTH
TYNE
DOGGER
GERMAN BIGHT
IRISH SEA
HUMBER
SHANNON
THAMES
FASTNET
LUNDY
DOVER
WIGHT
SOLE
PLYMOUTH
PORTLAND
FINISTERRE
BISCAY

COASTAL STATIONS
Fig. 7.

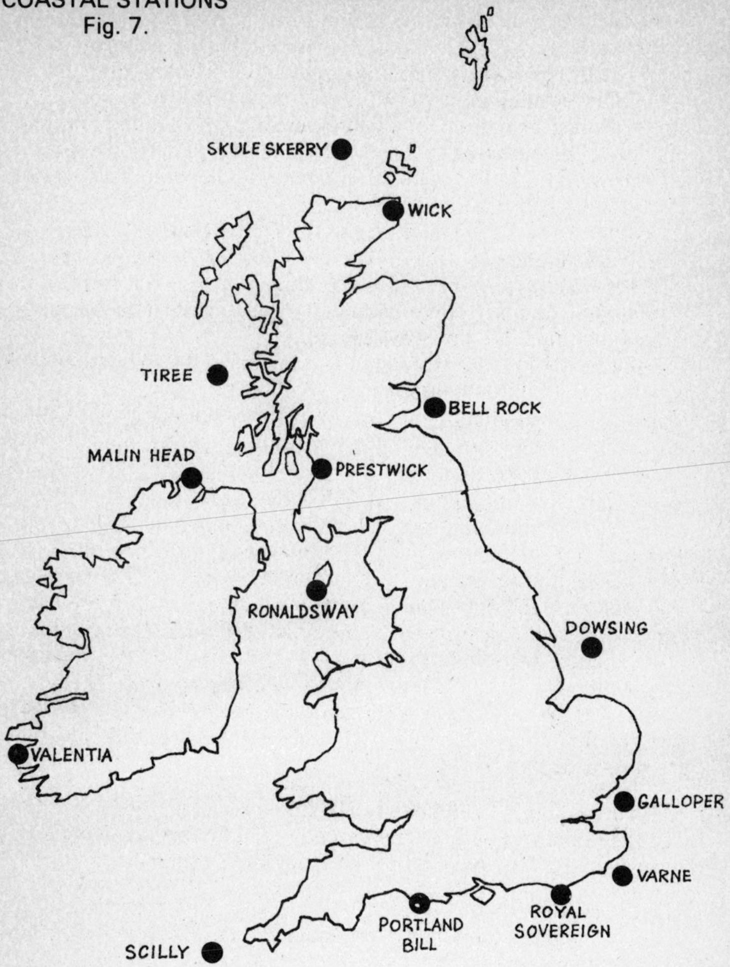

SHIPPING FORECASTS AND COASTAL REPORT: These radio forecasts come on Radio 2 (Shipping) and Radio 4 (Inshore). They include gale warnings, a general synopsis of the weather, and area forecasts from Coastal Stations. They are designed for merchant shipping, and as they give sea forecasts, they are of limited use to people inland. However, as they cover the period 24 hours ahead, they do give a good indication of approaching bad weather. You do need to know which land or sea forecast area you are in, and in the case of yachtsmen, your nearest Coastal Station, (Figs. 6 and 7).

To make the best use of these forecasts you have to know which particular sea areas concern you, and which are the nearest Coastal Stations, (Fig. 7). This, plus the relevant wind direction and speed, can enable you to make a good guess about future weather in your area, inland.

See the Radio Times for details and times of these broadcasts, as they are subject to change.

TAPED TELEPHONE FORECASTS AND LOCAL MET. OFFICES: There are over thirty local weather stations in the U.K., and most local telephone exchanges receive from these stations a weather forecast which they put on tape.

You can receive this taped forecast by dialling the appropriate number, obtainable from the telephone directory. You can also dial the local Met. Offices, the number of which will be found in the 'Yellow Pages'. For far-away areas, you can obtain the local Met. Office number from Directory Enquiries, but remember that, even in the South East, the London Weather Centre can tell you about the weather in Snowdonia, if you ring up and ask.

These offices are frequently centred on airfields, and the local airfield will always be able, and usually willing, to give you the local forecast.

METEOROLOGICAL SERVICES

You can obtain a booklet giving details of all Weather Advice by writing to the Metrological Office, Bracknell, Berkshire, England.

GALE WARNINGS

A 'Gale' means that winds of 34 knots (Force 8), or gusts up to 43 knots are expected. Gale warnings are broadcast on Radio 2 as soon as the BBC receives them, and then repeated the following hour. A summary of gale warnings precedes each shipping forecast. Visual gale warnings are also hoisted, in the shape of cones. A down-pointing cone indicates a southerly gale and an upward-pointing cone a northerly gale, (Fig. 8). These cones are displayed prominently around the coast, on Coastguard Stations etc.

Fig. 8.

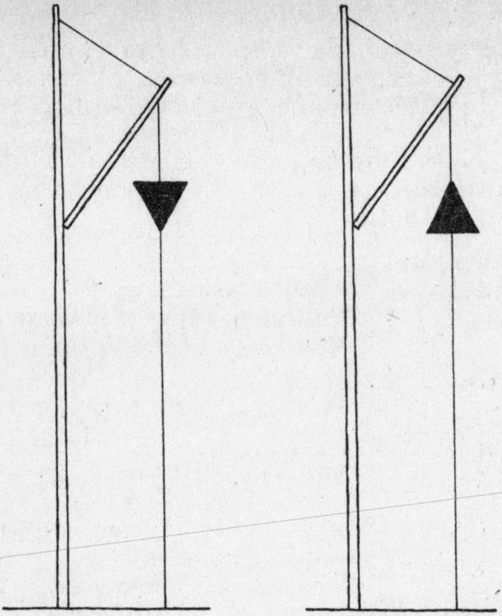

SOUTH CONE NORTH CONE

LOCAL KNOWLEDGE

No list of forecast sources can be complete without local information, and no outdoor man can afford to ignore any local weather advice he can collect from residents and institutions on the spot.

Try and make the source as authoritative as possible. The local airfield tower is a better guide than the landlord's corns, so start there, or the Police Station, the local outdoor shop, and so on. Farmers, fishermen and shepherds are out in all weathers and can give sound advice.

Don't neglect to ask for it.

So, as we can see, to obtain information on weather patterns is not difficult. Press, radio, T.V., local and national, plus local meteorological offices are all pumping out information. Gather up all the weather information you can. We still, however, have to interpret this information, and realise what it can mean to us, out there on the sea, moor or mountain.

Chapter 3

WEATHER TERMS

It has to be faced that weather forecasting—if in many respects an art—is increasingly based on science. It therefore employs common terms which have, for meteorological purposes, a strict definition.

Let us, therefore, just define here, what the forecasters mean when they use words like 'soon', 'gale', or 'imminent'.

1. **TIME:**

IMMINENT:	Within 6 hours of warning
SOON:	Within 6 to 12 hours of warning
LATER:	After 12 hours of warning

2. **GALE FORCE:**

GALE:	Wind 34 knots or more, or a wind with 43 knot gusts
SEVERE GALE:	Wind 41 knots or more, or a wind with 52 knot gusts
STORM:	Wind 48 knots or more, or a wind with gusts up to 61 knots

Wind forces are usually given on the Beaufort Scale (Fig. 3).

3. **WIND FORCES:**

Inland, the forecast uses different terms to describe wind.

TERM	BEAUFORT SCALE	SPEED
CALM	0	Nil
LIGHT	1–3	1 to 10 knots
MODERATE	4	11 to 16 knots
FRESH	5	17 to 21 knots
STRONG	6–7	22 to 33 knots
GALE	8	34 to 40 knots

Remember to note the temperature when considering wind. A light wind on a below-freezing day can make for very severe weather, and a strong wind makes it even nastier.

4. **VISIBILITY:**

GOOD:	More than five nautical miles
MODERATE:	Two to five nautical miles
POOR:	1,100 yards to two nautical miles
FOG:	Less than 1,100 yards

A nautical mile is 2027 yards; a land mile is 1760 yards.

A sea mile, therefore, is longer than a land mile.

The above terms are used at sea. Inland the fog density gets finer definition.

MIST:	Visibility 1,100 yards down to 200 yards
FOG:	Visibility below 200 yards
DENSE FOG:	Less than 50 yards

5. **PRECIPITATION:**

Generally this means rain, hail, drizzle, sleet, snow or any fall-out. The word 'Fair', to describe the weather means simply that nothing much is happening, and is now seldom used in forecasts.

6. **PRESSURE:**

In forecasts the pressure is given in millibars, from each coastal station, or at the centre of each weather system.

You should note (1) the variations between each centre and (2) the degree and rate of change in pressure.

The forecast will tell you what the pressure is doing, usually in the following terms:

STEADY:	Change less than .lmb. in 3 hours
RISING (or falling) slowly:	Change 1 to 1.5mb. last 3 hours
RISING (or falling):	1.6 to 3.5mb. in last 3 hours
RISING (or falling) quickly:	3.6 to 6.0mb. in last 3 hours
RISING (or falling) very rapidly:	More than 6.0mb. in last 3 hours

We shall discuss what all these terms mean to you, in weather, in future chapters.

Chapter 4

DEPRESSIONS, FRONTS AND ANTI-CYCLONES

The terms employed in Chapter 2 are all collected together to describe the weather, of which the two chief manifestations are Depressions (or lows) and Anti-cyclones (or highs). Let us now go over these two and get a firm idea of how these weather features usually affect us.

1. **DEPRESSIONS**: This can also be described as a 'low' or, less often, as a 'cyclone'. Please note that in this sense it means only a weak pressure centre, and not a tearing hurricane. The word 'cyclone' is used as the reverse of 'anti-cyclone'.

During a depression, in the Northern Hemisphere, pressure falls, and the winds blowing into the low pressure area circle in an anti-clockwise direction. (In the Southern Hemisphere they circle in a clockwise one). Remember low barometric pressure indicates a depression.

Depressions can be very large, quite big enough to cover the whole of the U.K.

In most depressions, the rain and clouds tend to come over in a series of **troughs** and **fronts.**

Winds vary in intensity according to the gradient between one isobar and the next, or the gradient in a series of isobars. If the pressure falls sharply, the winds will be strong. Close isobars indicate strong winds as close contour lines indicate a steep slope.

In the U.K., depressions normally come in from the Atlantic, moving from west to east. They bring, therefore, clouds, rain and winds; in other words changeable, if not especially cold, weather. When pressure is low, the air flowing in, circulates and moves in towards the centre. At the centre of the depression, the air rises, cools, and the water in the air condenses to form clouds which in turn lead to rain.

BUYS BALLOT LAW

Buys Ballot Law, said to be the only infallible rule in forecasting, states that if you want to locate the direction of the low, you stand with your back to the wind and the centre of the depression will lie on your left-hand side. In the Southern Hemisphere the low will be on the right-hand side. Remember that the winds will not blow directly into the low, but are skewed off by the rotation of the earth. (Fig. 9).

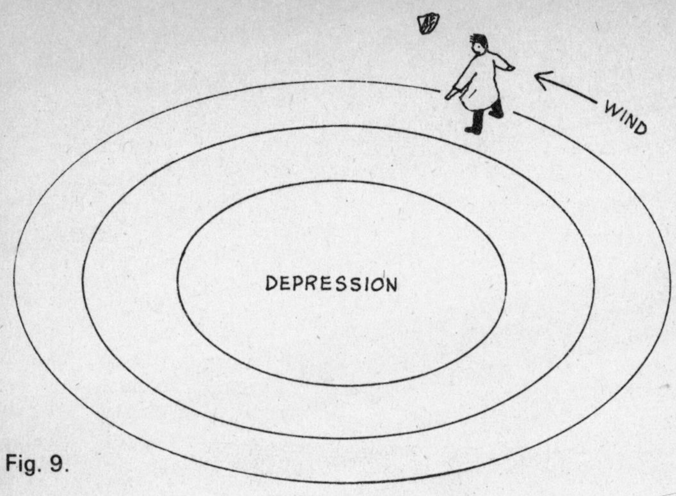

Fig. 9.

BUYS - BALLOT'S LAW

FRONTS

A 'front' is the frontier line between an area of warm air and an area of cold air, or vice-versa, and marks the edges of two air masses of different origin. The cold air will fall, and the warm air will rise over the cold air, (Fig. 10). This rising of the warm air causes clouds and rain.

In a 'warm front' the air temperature changes from cold to warm as the warm front passes through, while in a 'cold front' the reverse happens. The air changes from warm to cold.

The ascent of warm air over cold, or the undercutting of a warm air mass by cold air only happens when the air masses are moving at different speeds. If the air masses are stationary, the "fronts" are ill-defined, and semi-stationary.

ANTI-CYCLONES (Highs)

In an anti-cyclone, the pressure is high, the winds light, and the weather *generally* fine and warm. Anti-cyclones are slow moving, and you can get a cloudy anti-cyclone. They don't always mean fine weather.

The winds circulate clockwise (the reverse of the cyclonic or 'low'), in the Northern Hemisphere and anti-clockwise in the Southern Hemisphere.

Frequently, you will experience a 'ridge of high pressure'

Fig. 10.

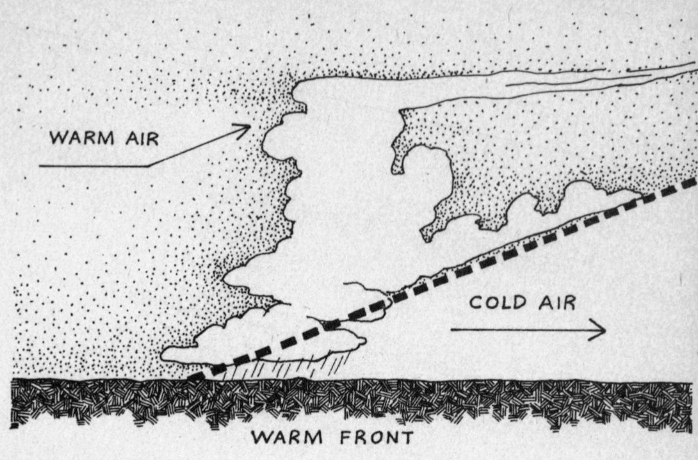

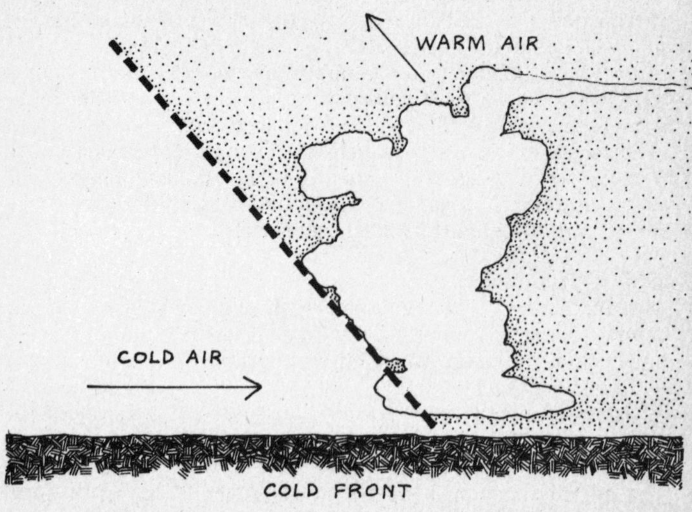

between two lows, in which for a brief period, perhaps a few hours, perhaps a day or two, the skies clear, the winds drop, and the sun comes out. Then the 'ridge' passes and the clouds come in again.

Away from the centre of an anti-cyclone the winds increase. An anti-cyclone centred over, say, the Azores, can mean fine summer weather for England, but with high, force 4–6 winds, and in winter the Azores high can bring cloud and drizzle. So remember to note the *centre* of the anti-cyclone, for in winter, a Scandinavian-centred anti-cyclone can bring very cold weather.

AN OCCLUSION

An Occlusion is caused by the combining of a warm and cold front. It can make for prolonged outbursts of rain, then showers, and perhaps thunderstorms. Occlusions are slow moving and take time to clear. (Fig. 11).

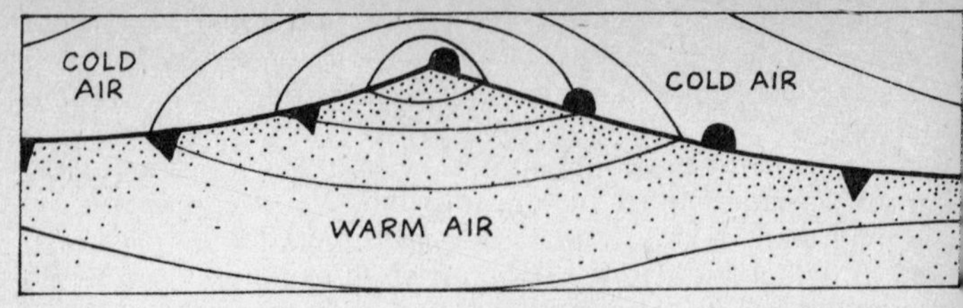

A SMALL WAVE IS FORMED IN A FRONT

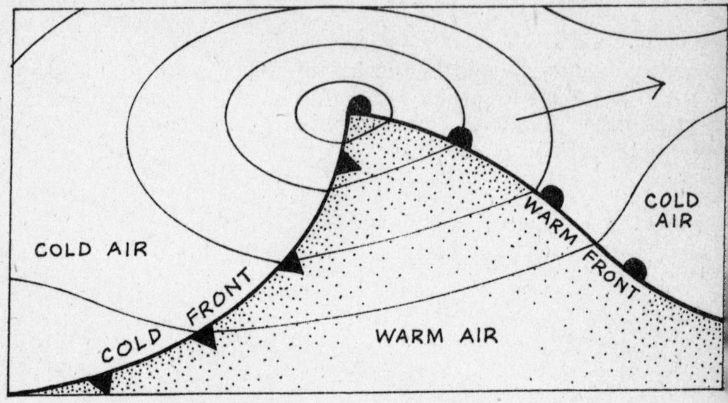

THIS DEVELOPS INTO A WARM AND A COLD FRONT

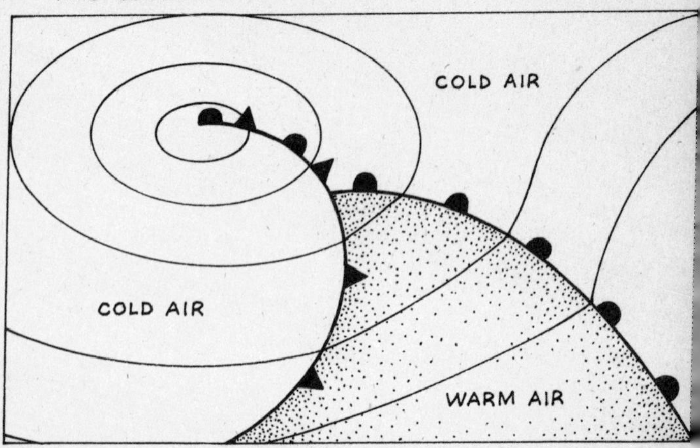

THE COLD FRONT OVERTAKES THE WARM FRONT. AN OCCLUSION

Fig. 11.

Chapter 5

CLOUDS

In the short term clouds provide one of the best indicators we have to changes in the weather. At sea or in the mountains the approach of a cloud mass can be observed from a great distance, and coupled with other signs, such as barometric and temperature changes, they can give a good guide to the weather over the next few hours. Remember that it is a *combination* of factors that tell you about the weather; pressure, temperature, wind direction etc., not just one isolated factor on its own.

It is however, only fair to point out that with clouds, as in other weather features, even a strong indication is uncertain. Lowering rain clouds may promise rain, but it may not rain on you. High winds or local variations can bring bad weather on to your position or carry it past.

This said, clouds are a most useful guide to the amateur forecaster, and an endless topic for speculation.

WHAT IS A CLOUD

Clouds are formed, essentially, by the condensation of moisture laden air. As air rises, it cools, the pressure decreases, and clouds form, as the air reaches its dew point. The usual process is that the sun heats the ground, the ground heats the air, the air rises, bubbles through the higher, cooler, air and clouds form.

Air is forced or drawn upwards by various causes. Most frequently over land the air rises by convection, drawn up by the tendency of warm air to rise, heated by the sun's rays reflected off the earth, but the main cause of clouds is the dynamic effect of 'fronts', and these frontal clouds can cover large areas.

In mountain country the shape of the rising ground forces the air currents up, and cloud forms on the tops of the hills. On fine, clear days, many mountains, especially on islands, carry a feathery streamer of cloud on their leeward side.

The degree of cloud cover, and the type of cloud depends on such local geographic variations, and the effect of the prevailing pressure systems. Different types of front produce different types of cloud.

TYPES OF CLOUD

Clouds are defined in two ways: by their height, and by their shape, and can be divided into about ten groups.

Starting from the top, these go as follows:

	Height	
HIGH	18,000 feet plus	CIRRUS
MEDIUM	8,000 to 18,000 feet	ALTO
LOW	Below 8,000 feet	STRATUS

The next definition is by shape, and this again falls into three main types:

FEATHER type	CIRROFORM
LAYER type	STRATIFORM
HEAP type	CUMULIFORM

Fig. 12.

CUMULUS

Given these two definitions, we can describe by height and shape many different sorts of clouds, from the high feather-like Cirrus to such combinations as Stratocumulus (layer clouds at low height), and Cirrostratus (layer clouds at great height).

Cumulus clouds are common cloud forms and have two main types: As they are common, lets look at them first.

1. **CUMULUS**

This is a low, horizontal based cloud that can climb up to a great height. It has vertical development through all layers. Fair weather cumulus consists of cotton-wool type clouds, well separated, in the Alto range. Medium Cumulus is dark and flat at the base, towering up in white pinnacles. It is a convection cloud. Cumulus cloud generally indicates good weather, unless it is thickening (Fig. 12). The significant thing about Cumulus clouds is their towering vertical development.

CUMULONIMBUS

Fig. 13.

1. CUMULONIMBUS

This is a large, thick cloud, growing up from a low height, often anvil shaped at the top, and combined with Anvil Cirrus. It is a thunder cloud, and brings rain, squalls and lightning risk. Cumulonimbus is a convection cloud, and occurs during cold fronts covering a small area. (Fig. 13).

While we are dealing with Cumulonimbus, we might look at the Nimbus cloud.

NIMBUS

Nimbus means rain, so to the above we should add the nimbus form of cloud, notably Nimbostratus (layered grey clouds from medium to high), which is usually grouped with the Alto range. With Nimbostratus it is usually raining or snowing already. There is a saying *"I have a little dog and call him Nimbus because he is always making puddles"*.

Nimbus clouds are noted for their dark, menacing appearance and Cumulonimbus is always associated with thunderstorms and bad weather. Nimbus clouds are the ones to worry about. Nimbostratus only occurs with fronts, and does not have an 'anvil'.

Fig. 14. CIRRUS

CIRRUS

Cirrus clouds are light, very fine, delicate clouds, and at a great height are formed of ice crystals. They are spread thinly over the sky, and are frequently shredded. (Fig. 14). Although attractive, they usually mean that unsettled weather is on the way in the shape of an occlusion, with rising winds, the Cirrus clouds thickening, becoming milky in appearance, and rain clouds moving in later. Dispersing Cirrus, on the other hand, means a warming of the upper air, and the arrival of good weather. Check if the barometer is falling.

Two other types, or sub-types of Cirrus cloud are Cirrocumulus and Cirrostratus.

CIRROCUMULUS

This formation is often referred to as a 'mackerel sky'. The clouds are high—as are all Cirrus clouds—and puffy, quite small, and smeared across the sky in bands, rippled like the sand on a beach. This can be taken as a broad hint that the weather is unsettled—showers, and some thunder are a possibility. The wind may increase later, say, within twelve hours. (Fig. 15).

Fig. 15. CIRROCUMULUS

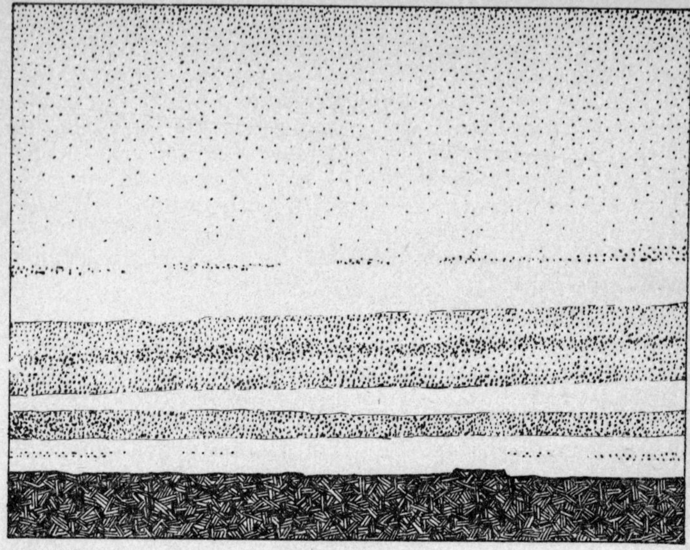

Fig. 16.

CIRROSTRATUS

The clouds, again at a great height, cover the sky in a thin, smooth layer. This layer is composed of ice crystals and is sometimes the cause of a halo about the sun or a ring around the moon. Indeed Cirrostratus is sometimes so thin that only the 'halo' tells you it is there. It indicates wind, and the probability of rain especially if the barometer is falling, and probably the approach of a warm front. (Fig. 16).

ANVILCIRRUS

Anvilcirrus is associated with Cumulonimbus. It is caused by ice crystals fluttering and blowing out at great height. This gives rise to the 'anvil cloud' usually indicating high winds and storm. As the cloud rises, the high altitude winds push the cloud down into the characteristic anvil shape. Broken weather, with winds and squalls usually follows. So if you see anvil cirrus and cumulonimbus approaching, watch out. (Fig. 17).

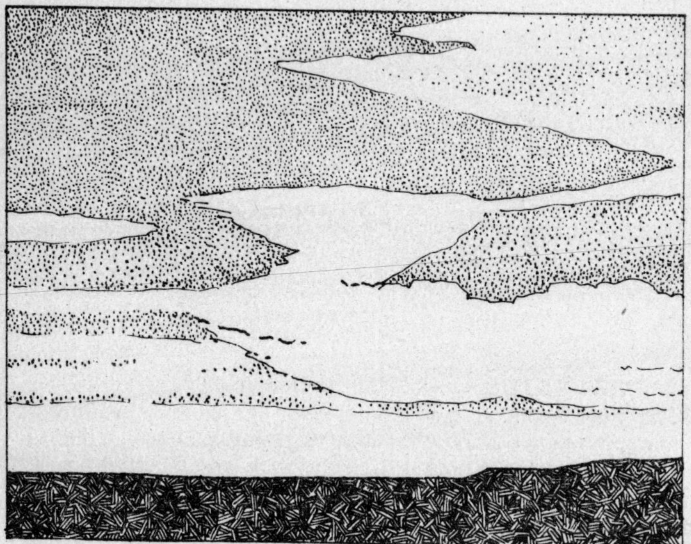

Fig. 17. ANVIL CIRRUS

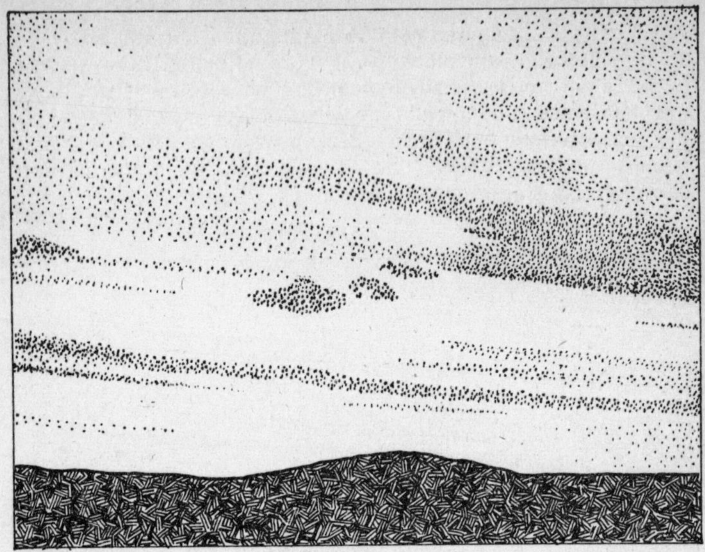

Fig. 18. ALTOSTRATUS

ALTOSTRATUS

The next layer of clouds—between 8000 and 18000 feet, medium clouds, is the Alto layer, Altostratus, and Altocumulus.

The first point to note is that, obviously enough, these clouds are never so high nor so thin as the Cirrus ones.

Cirrostratus clouds frequently lower to become Altostratus. Altostratus clouds completely blanket the sky, blotting out sun and moon, but are so thick that no 'halo' effect is visible. These clouds indicate rain, or possibly snow if the temperature is low enough. (Fig. 18).

ALTOCUMULUS

This has been described as a fair weather cloud. Altocumulus often occurs when bad weather is clearing away, when the large fluffy clouds slowly disperse to let the sun through. Composed of water droplets, the lower parts of Altocumulus can be dark, and these large clouds frequently send deep shadows over the earth below. All in all though, a good sight, in most cases, especially broken Altocumulus, but beware when altocumulus clouds mass together, as muggy, cloudy weather may result.(Fig. 19).

Fig. 19. ALTOCUMULUS

Fig. 20. STRATUS

STRATUS

Finally, among these main cloud groups, we have the low altitude stratus clouds. These are the clouds that give the U.K. its dull, grey, cold 'typical winter's day' look. On high ground they lead to hill fog and, conversely, low cloud or fog can lift up to become Stratus. (Fig. 20).

STRATOCUMULUS

This is low, flat based cloud, rising up in heaps. Stratocumulus is a cloud formation usually seen in winter, and usually indicates bad weather. (Fig. 21).

There are two types of Stratocumulus. "Air mass" Stratocumulus, heaped white clouds, may only give a little drizzle but "Frontal" Stratocumulus is associated with "fronts", and may, seen from a hilltop, indicate the approach of a storm which may be overstating the obvious but is a point to bear in mind. Watch the clouds, they can tell you what is coming.

As we have seen, clouds generally indicate a change in the weather, often for the worse, but they do have more beneficial effects. A cloudy night, especially in winter, will be warmer than a clear one, as the earth, warmed during the day, will have the heat sealed in by the cloud layer. Without the cloud, a frosty night is probable, and the cloud acts as a blanket. If the clouds are getting lower, the weather will deteriorate, hence the phrase, a 'lowering sky'. High clouds moving rapidly indicate changeable weather.

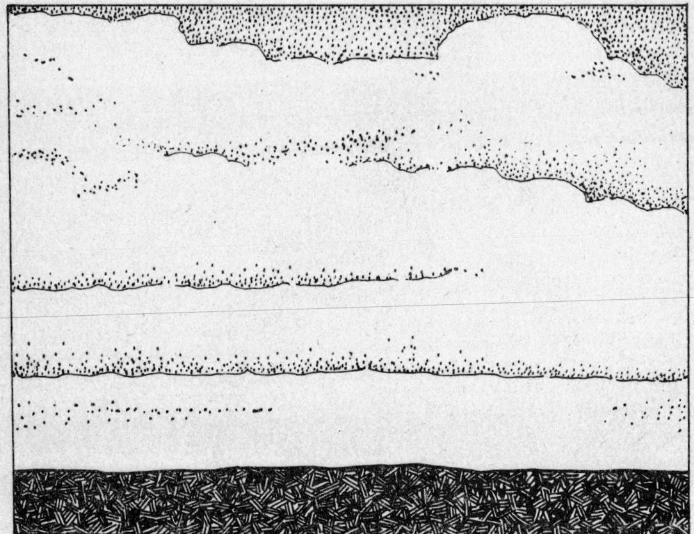

Fig. 21. STRATOCUMULUS

Clouds do give the outdoor man some good tips on the weather. A 'ring around the moon' usually means rain. The higher the clouds (usually) the better the outlook, unless of course the clouds are thickening. Low cloud in the early dawn, or mist in the valleys, usually, in summer anyway, gives the hope of a fine day later. 'Rain before seven—sun by eleven' as the countryfolk used to say.

But remember, in this as in all weather study, you have to consider a combination of factors; pressure, temperature, humidity and the trend of weather over the previous days.

Study the clouds, though, always. They are signposts in the sky.

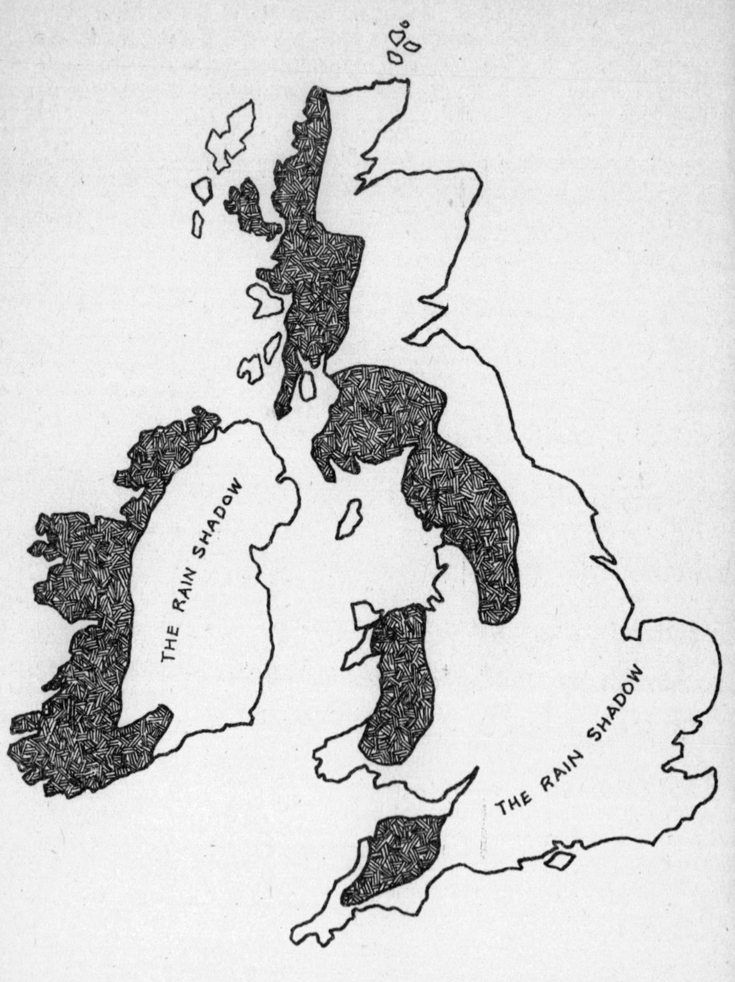

Fig. 22.

RAIN AND WIND

Rain and wind, separately, can and must be endured by outdoor people. It is when they come together that the weather conditions are frequently intolerable. The amateur forecaster should know something about wind and rain, in relation to his own area, for both are greatly influenced by local topography.

WIND

The first thing to establish is the direction of the *prevailing wind;* that is the direction from which the wind most often comes.

In the U.K. the prevailing wind is south-westerly, from the Atlantic. It is, after its passage over the ocean, a wet wind, and can bring with it clouds and rain, particularly in winter. The other summer wind is from the south-east, across the Continent of Europe. In summer this wind, blowing across land, has become warm and dry.

In winter, while the same winds blow, the effect is different. The south-westerly winds are the warm winds, warmed by the ocean, and the easterly winds, flowing from Russia, are bitterly cold.

AIR TEMPERATURES

This situation becomes clearer if you understand the way in which air becomes warm.

The earth's heat comes from the sun, and the sea is slow to heat, and slow to cool. The land, on the other hand, warms up quickly, and cools quickly.

The air—and therefore the winds—draws little heat from the sun directly. The sun warms land and sea, and the air picks up reflected warmth, while passing over them.

In the winter then, the sea retains much of the heat it absorbed in the summer, while land temperatures plummet.

THE 'RAIN SHADOW'

When moisture-laden air reaches land and comes against mountains, it has to rise. As it rises, the pressure drops, and the air cools, the moisture condensing into clouds, which eventually fall as rain. This precipitation frequently occurs on the windward side of mountains, the side facing the prevailing wind. The area without rain, beyond the mountains, is said to lie in the 'rain shadow'. (Fig. 22).

In the U.K. and Eire, with the prevailing wet westerlies, we get more rain on the western coasts and mountains, such as Snowdonia and the Western Highlands.

WIND SPEEDS

Wind speeds are usually expressed in knots—or sea miles per hour. A scale frequently employed, especially by mariners, is the Beaufort Scale (Fig. 3), devised by Admiral Beaufort during the age of Sail. He calculated windforce by observation (the effect of wind on sails) and drew up his scale from Force 1 (becalmed) to Force 12 (Heaven help you!) and calculated the effect such winds would have on a 'well found man of war'. Subsequentally other people calculated his scale back into wind speeds, after the invention of the anemometer had enabled them to do so.

The outdoor man, in a boat or not, has to gauge exactly what wind force is acceptable for his area and activity. Dinghy and offshore cruising yachtsmen need to become cautious over about Force 4. A sustained Force 4 can make for pleasant sailing, but if the wind is rising, there will be gusts up to Force 6 or 7 (near gale), and these can put him in difficulties. Small boat sailors should therefore be aware of the signs of a Force 4 wind and modify their plans when they appear. The Southampton Weather Centre now issues a Force 6 warning for cruising yachtsmen. On tidal waters, the effect on the sea is worse if you get 'wind against tide', which can make for turbulent water.

Inland, Force 5 to 6 is bearable, unless you are climbing in exposed situations. There have been cases of climbers being blown over cliffs by Force 8 gusts, and above Force 5 the hiker or hill-trekker should keep away from crests, and pick up what shelter he can from the lee of hills or woods.

'BACKING' AND 'VEERING'

When the wind direction is changing in a clockwise direction (from left to right) it is said to veer. When it is moving in an anti-clockwise direction it is said to 'back'.

Winds 'back' ahead of depressions or 'lows', and increase in strength, ahead of fronts. Winds 'veer' with the passage of fronts. The 'veering' winds usually drop, although there may be squalls.

It is reasonable to say that a 'backing' wind is increasing and a 'veering' wind is falling, but as always with local variations. (Fig. 23).

PRECIPITATION

Precipitation is the collective term for rain, hail, snow or sleet. Official forecasts sometimes mention that there is 'precipitation' in sight.

The type of precipitation is governed by the temperature. Below 0° C (32° F) you will get snow, and you can get snow in the hills in early summer if you are high enough for it to become that cold. As a rough guide, temperature falls about 3° C with every 1000 ft. of height, so what falls as rain in the valley may be snow on the top, and sleet or hail in between.

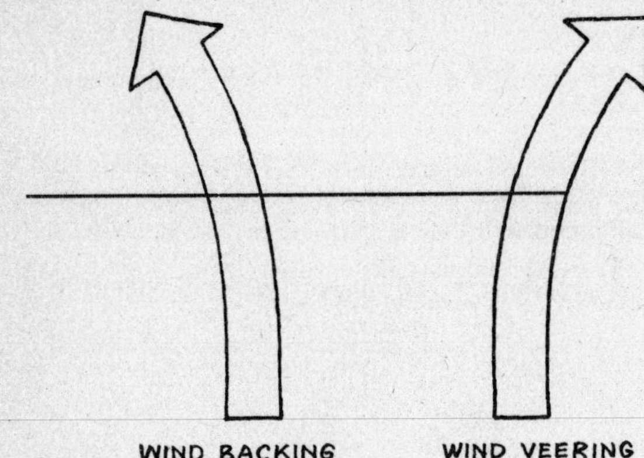

Fig. 23.

RAINFALL AND CLOUDS

Apart from the steady rain or drizzle that falls from a grey, stratus-covered sky, certain clouds bring rain with them, and this rain can often be seen approaching, at least in time for you to get the anorak on, or the tent up.

Cumulonimbus clouds usually bring heavy showers, often with thunder and lightning. (See previous chapter).

Nimbostratus clouds alone usually mean it's raining already, while thickening Cumulus clouds can bring showers.

WIND AND WEATHER

As you will have noticed by now, the wind has a very significant part to play in the local weather pattern, and as a general rule, certain winds, as often as not, bring certain kinds of weather with them. (Fig. 24).

If, therefore, you can identify the wind force and direction, it will, if linked with other information, enable you to make a calculated guess at the weather over the next few hours or days.

Since most outdoor activities take place in summer, let us look at summer winds first. (Fig. 24).

NORTH
COLD AND SHOWERY
NORTH WEST
CLOUDY AND SHOWERY
NORTH EAST
COLD AND SHOWERY
WEST
CLOUDY
EAST
COLD AND DRY
SOUTH WEST
WARM AND CLOUDY
SOUTH EAST
WARM AND DRY
SOUTH
WARM AND DRY
Fig. 24.

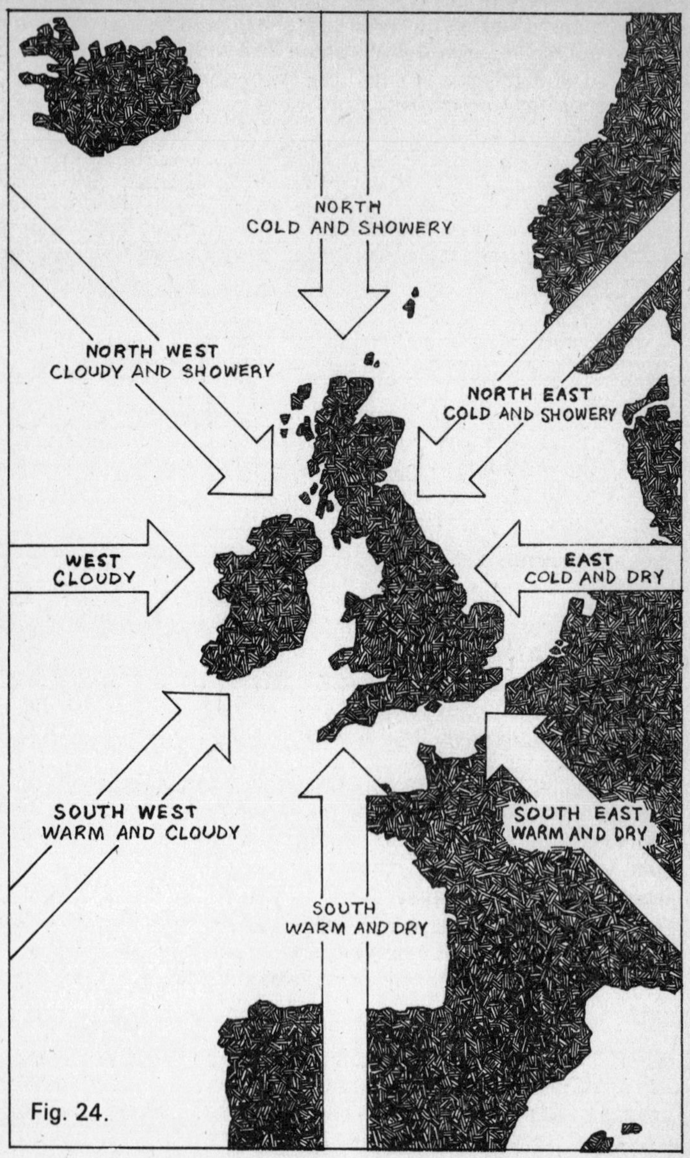

SUMMER WINDS (Fig. 24).

Wind Direction: (where it's coming from)	*Brings:*
NORTH	Cool weather especially at night; rain, or fog haze.
NORTH-EAST	Colder winds, but fine clear weather, but showers in East.
EAST	Warm dry winds, clear skies, but cool in East.
SOUTH-EAST SOUTH	Gives the U.K. those summer days and heat waves. Maybe thunder in South later.
SOUTH-WEST	Very warm but cloudy, after long sea trip.
WEST	Warm and wet, hill cloud.
NORTH-WEST	Cooler days and nights, heavy showers.

WINTER WINDS

In winter, while the weather generally is worse, the effects of individual winds is quite marked.

WIND DIRECTION	*EFFECT*
NORTH	Very cold, rain and snow.
NORTH-EAST	Very cold, but probably clear.
EAST	Cold, rain, sleet, snow on high ground.
SOUTH-EAST SOUTH	These winds are not common in winter, worse luck, but clear, cold, brisk days come with these winds.
SOUTH-WEST	Cloudy, drizzle, low cloud and fog, wet.
WEST	Dull, wet weather.
NORTH-WEST	Showers, frost, clear spells.

Remember that you must take other information into account, pressure and temperature particularly. Some areas get a lot of shelter from the wind, and are therefore drier and warmer.

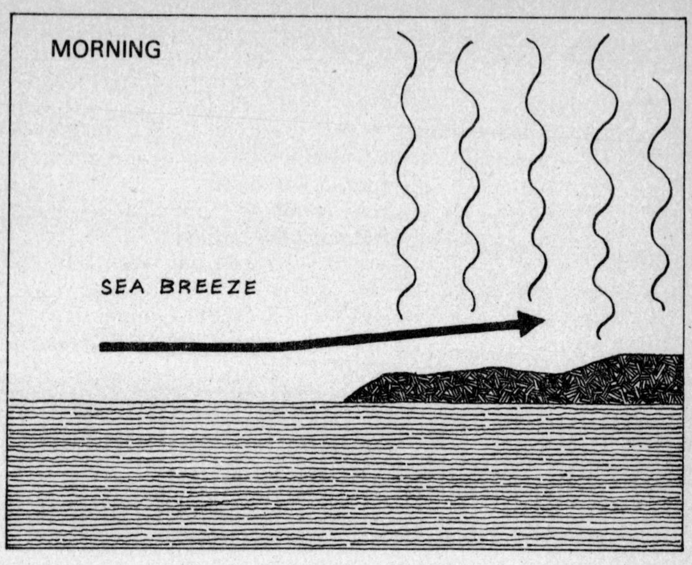

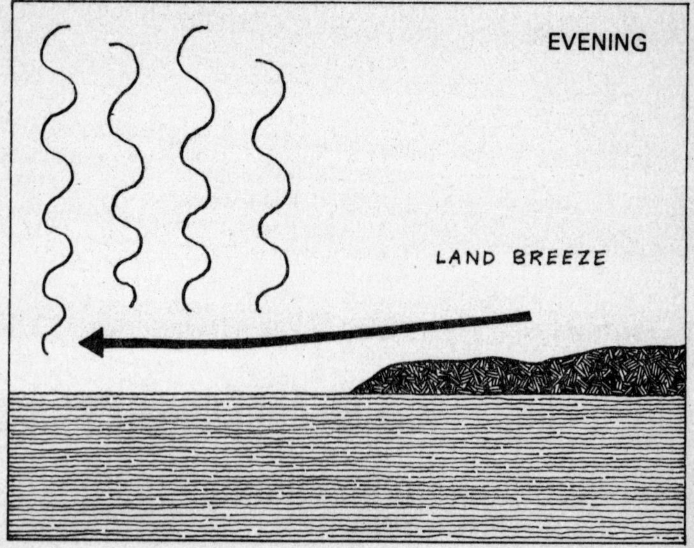

Fig. 25.

LAND AND SEA BREEZES

In summer, on the coast, the yachtsman or holiday-maker, will frequently experience breezes off the sea or land. These winds, local in effect, are caused by convection currents, that is, the effect on the air of the sun's heat rising.

In the morning, when the sun comes up, the earth warms quickly, and warms the air above it, which then rises.

Cooler air from the sea flows in to fill the gap, and a pleasant cool 'sea breeze' is often blowing by mid-morning. This can frequently increase the coastal wind speed and alters the wind direction relative to the coast.

In the evening the reverse happens, the sun goes down, the earth cools, and the breeze flows off the land, out to sea.

Between these two, at dawn and dusk, you often get a lull, when the wind drops right away, to the delight of parachutists, and the disgust of yachtsmen. (Fig. 25).

Chapter 7

WEATHER SAWS AND SAYINGS

In the U.K. with a population obsessed with the weather, there is, naturally enough, a host of sayings associated with the climate, and usually attempting some sort of forecast. Many of them are probably rubbish, but some seem to work, at least part of the time, and are worth knowing.

To begin with let's try the best known:

Red sky at night, shepherd's delight
Red sky in the morning, shepherd's warning.

This is possibly true, since the red sky is the sun shining on clouds and a red western evening sky means that the sky is clearing. Yellow sunsets usually mean unsettled weather.

Rain before seven, Sun by eleven.

Often comes true, unless the sky is full of Stratus.

If on St. Swithun's it do rain,
For forty days shall do the same.

St. Swithun's Day is 15th July, and the Saint is buried, incidentally, in Winchester Cathedral. A survey by the Met. Office 'since records were kept' reveals that there is no basis for this one.

Shiny morning, Cloudy day.

Frequently true. How often have you rolled out of the sleeping bag to a clear blue dawn, and had it cloudy and raining by mid-morning? The word 'shiny' is the clue. A dazzling dawn often deteriorates.

Rain from the East,
Means a day's rain at least.

In the winter time, this is probably true, with rain or snow, depending on the temperature.

Mackerel sky and mare's tails,
Make tall ships wear small sails.

Quite true, as mackeral sky (Cirrocumulus) is an indication of unsettled weather, with squalls, and a possibility of an increase in wind within 12 hours.

Long foretold, long past,
Short notice soon past,
Quick rise from below,
Certain sign of stronger blow.

This is a not-so-old-saying that relates to the barometer. It is fair to say that a gradual rise or fall in the barometer is a surer indication of good or bad weather than a quick change. It is also true that while a sudden drop in pressure indicates poor weather, a quick rise often falls again, and the 'low' is deeper than before, with higher winds.

The same barometric theory is covered in:

When the glass falls low,
Prepare for a blow.
When it slowly rises high,
Lofty sails you may fly.

Note the 'slowly rises'. A fast-rising barometer, probably means bad weather later, for a quick rise will often fall again.

Ring Around the Moon

A ring around the moon, or a haze over the moon's face, usually means rain and cloud.

As we have noticed, winter weather, good or bad, often has causes directly opposite to summer weather. The same winds for example, have different effects.

For example:

When the wind is in the East,
It brings no good to man or beast.

In winter this is quite true, for in winter east winds are bitter. In the summer, the east and north-easterlies bring warm dry air from the Continent.

Less pretty, but quite accurate is:

The farther the sight—the nearer the rain.

There is a lot of truth in this. Where we live, on a hill overlooking the Thames Valley, a quick glance out of the window in the morning is a good guide (usually) to the day's weather. If there is sun where we are, in the garden, but mist obscures the valley, the day is usually fine, but if one can pick out the craft on the river, it will usually cloud over and rain before the day is out. This is not very scientific, but in the eight years we have lived here, it has proved pretty accurate.

The same seems to hold good for other parts as well. When we were on Dartmoor, people would say that if you could see the Dewerstone it was going to rain, and if you couldn't, then it was raining already.

FOLK BELIEFS

This leads on to more jolly facets of weather lore.

SEAWEED

Every year, as boys, we would bring home from the seaside, a long piece of kelp, firmly believing it would turn soft and wet when rain was due and become stiff when the sun shone. (Fig. 27).

In fact, it set like a board, and became brittle. Yet on the train the other day, there was a crowd of children returning from an outing, each clutching a piece of seaweed in the same belief.

It's not only not true, it doesn't work and we can find no basis for the idea at all. It's fun for children, though.

Fig. 27.

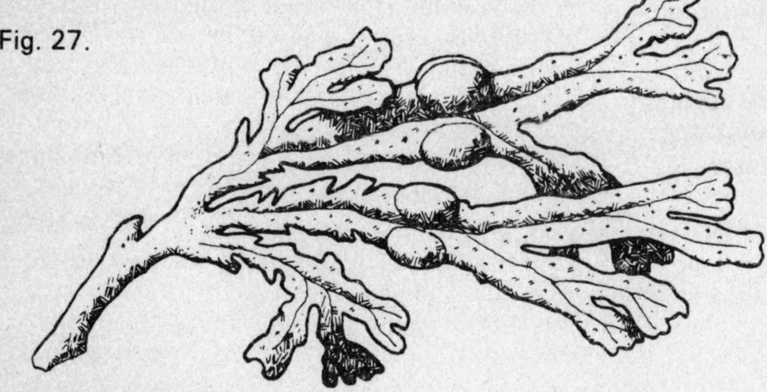

PINE CONES

We have before us two pine cones. The weather is dry(ish) and the glass steady(ish).

According to legend the pine cones (wily creatures) clamp up tight, when rain is due. Our particular cones seem to be disgruntled about something, since one is tight shut and the other is wide open. So either we have unco-operative cones or by a split vote they are indicating variable weather. So, remember, you need two cones! (Fig. 28).

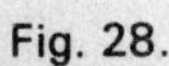

Fig. 28.

COWS

Popular belief has it that if you see all the cows laying down, it's going to rain. Cows, crafty creatures, lie down just to preserve a patch of dry grass to lie on.

Cows do seem to flop down in bad weather (so do we, come to that—on the sofa before the box, to be exact). Anyway, if you promise not to tell the RSPCA we can tell you how to put this bovine habit to good use when caught out in the rain. Find your friendly neighbourhood cow, give it a gentle boot in the tail, and as it lumbers up, whack your groundsheet down fast and have a dry couch for the night. Mind you, the miserable beast will moo outside the flysheet all night, but you can't have it all ways!

The same story is, we believe, told about elephants, and probably polar bears.

As you can see, as with most aspects of weather lore, it's best to take it with a pinch of salt; (salt, incidentally, is supposed to get damp when it's going to rain).

But enough of this. Let us now try and apply this information to your own activities, and the preparation of your own forecasts.

Chapter 8

READING A WEATHER CHART

To the layman, the weather chart is a fearsome sight, covered with signs and symbols, but don't worry. Remember how puzzling an O.S. map was when you first saw one. (If an O.S. map still puzzles you, read the Venture Guide *"Map and Compass"*).

Study the weather maps in the press and you will soon begin to see how weather maps are made up.

CONVENTIONAL WEATHER SIGNS

ISOBARS

Isobars link points of equal pressure, as a contour line links points of equal height.

Direction front is moving:

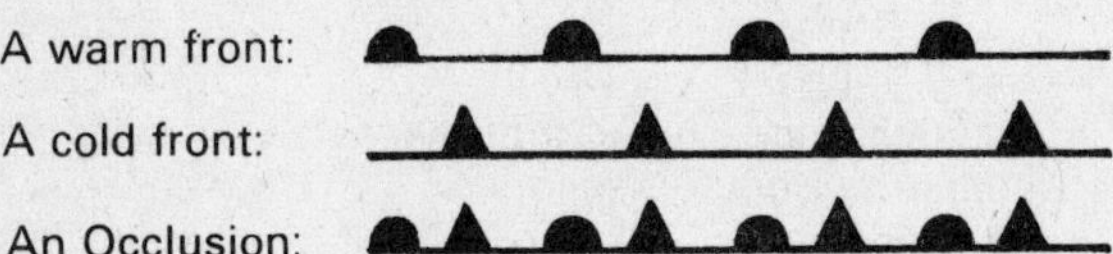

Isobars also carry the pressure level.

Remember that if the isobars are close together it means high winds and if far apart it means light ones.

'Lows' and 'Highs' are illustrated in Fig. 29.

Remember that winds blow from high into low pressure areas.

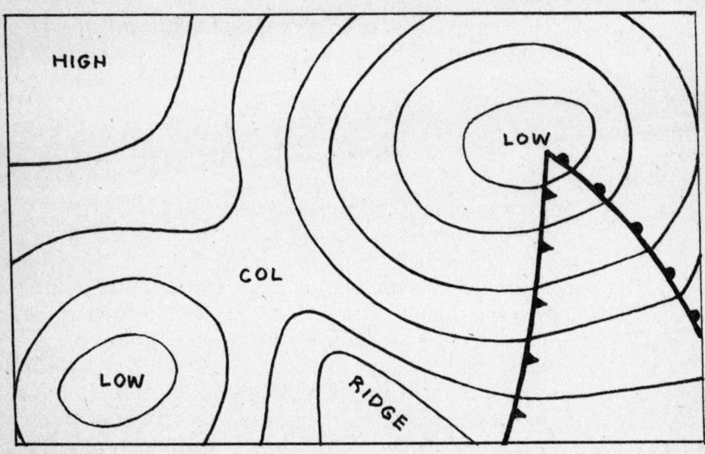

Fig. 29.

As you can see, the weather chart gives a lot of useful information, even to the amateur.

BEAUFORT NOTATION

Admiral Beaufort left a series of abbreviations for weather conditions, which are still used today, especially in Press forecasts. You can see below some of the most important.

WEATHER	*NOTATION*
Blue sky	b
Broken cloud	bc
Cloudy	d
Fog	F
Gale	G
Lightning	l
Overcast	o
Rain	r
Snow	s
Thunder	t

In addition, modern weather maps use symbols instead of, or as well as the Beaufort notation.

For example:

Rain	=	●	Snow	=	✱
Drizzle	=	d, ●	Thunderstorms	=	[symbol]
Mist	=	═	Fog	=	≡

You will also notice that official weather maps are, apart from isobars etc., covered with little arrow-like symbols that look like this: (Fig. 32).

12 995

f

995 is tho barometric pressure = 995°
F is Beaufort notation = Fog
12 is the visibility = 12 sea miles.

The small circle at the top of the handle is the centre of the sea area, or marks the Coastal Station. The direction of the handle, or long arm, or arrow away from the circle, points to where the wind is coming *from*; in this case S.W. and the little bars jutting off like feathers indicate the wind force on the Beaufort scale. Each long bar is 2 points, so the above symbol, an arrow with 2½ bars, indicates a S.W, wind Force 5, *approximately.* To be quite accurate each little bar or fleche, is 10 knots of wind, and each half-bar (or half fleche) 5 knots. As the wind increases this moves gradually away from direct comparison with the Beaufort scale, but at winds up to 30 kts, they are very similar (Fig. 32).

Just to make it clearer here are a few more examples:

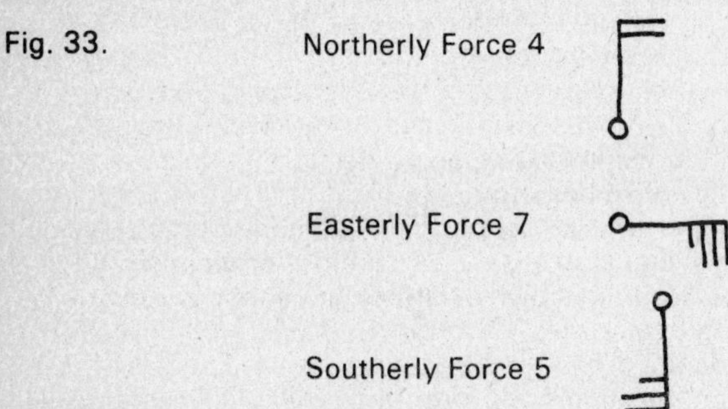

Fig. 33.

The bars or fleches project from the handle in the direction of the lowest pressure. If you apply Buys Ballot Law (Page 24) this, in the Northern Hemisphere puts them on the left-hand side, coming from the Station, or area centre.

Changeable winds would be illustrated as follows:

Wind S.E. Force 5 becoming S.W. Force 6, the little arrow giving the direction of the change.

Chapter 9

COMBATING THE WEATHER

"Some are weatherwise, and some are otherwise"

— Benjamin Franklin

The Chinese have a proverb about the bamboo. It bends in the storms, and it stands because it bends. It's a point worth remembering. There is nothing clever about going out in bad weather, and it is downright criminal to go out in bad weather without the proper knowledge, training and equipment.

You cannot fight the weather. It is foolish to try. Moreover, even relatively mild weather can prove decidedly unpleasant when you are away from home and out in it.

Certain types of weather can have certain effects on you.

HUMIDITY: Heat stroke is the danger in such weather. If the air is saturated with moisture, perspiration cannot evaporate from the skin and heat stroke may follow.

RAIN: If you are out in rain, and put on waterproofs, remember that you can get almost as wet under them from perspiration. When you take the waterproofs off after the rain, the sweat will cool and you can get a chill.

So, when you wear waterproofs, remember to let the air in, while keeping the rain out.

When camping, don't camp in stream beds if it looks like rain, or around low marshy ground. Avoid exposed hill sides and water meadows.

FROST: Clear, starry nights in winter, will lead to a drop in temperature, and a frost. Cloudy nights may not be so pretty but they are warmer. The clouds stop the warmth dispersing into the atmosphere. If the wind is allied to low temperatures, look out for frostbite on ear-lobes, fingers and toes.

WIND: The Rescue Services get a lot of calls every year, most of them unnecessary. Yachts at sea are often out in winds which are far from severe, but are in trouble through being over canvassed, or because beating the weather has exhausted the crew. Over *Force 4* be willing to reef and reduce canvas steadily as the wind increases—or don't go out at all.

WIND AND COLD AND WET: This combination can lead to hypothermia, or exposure. If you are out in these weather conditions, look out for the symptoms of hypothermia. A victim will fall behind, have slurred speech, or become excessively talkative, will become unco-operative, and eventually collapse. The treatment is to get him/her out of the wind and get them warm.

LOW TEMPERATURE AND WIND (WIND-CHILL): Low temperatures in themselves are no real problem if you are adequately clad, and keep moving. However, if the wind gets up, as can easily happen in cold, frosty weather, then the *effective* temperature is much lower than the air temperature. At, say −1°C a 20 mile an hour wind gives an *effective* temperature much below the true air temperature of − 1°C, and that can be lethal if you are not prepared for it. Your flesh can freeze. So, to be more mundane, can the water in your water-bottle, so take it into your tent. Below − 5°C pipes freeze and roads become icy.

Note also that water on roads freezes whenever the ground temperature falls to 0°C to − 1°C, and this can occur even though the true air temperature is higher, up to +5°C. So beware of icy roads when driving home tired after the weekend. The windscreen may not be icy, but the road surface can be.

LIGHTNING: High, dark cumulonimbus clouds can mean lightning. Get rid of or conceal metal objects, like ice axes or metal pack frames. Move off high ground, but stay away from solitary trees. Woods are good cover, but if you are in exposed country lie down in a hollow. Sit on your rubber mattress until the storm passes.

If you have grasped that different types of weather can present you with problems, then the problems can be anticipated and coped with.

CLOTHING

The outdoor man usually has to consider weight and comfort when he goes out of doors, whatever the weather. As he can probably not afford a range of clothing, he sticks to the same clothing whatever the weather.

This is not really bad, as the secret usually lies in having layers of clothing, rather than one thick windproof jacket.

Obviously one wears clothes to combat bad weather, and as few clothes as possible in good weather. A few do's and don'ts can be listed:

1. Do keep your head covered in cold weather—30% of the body heat loss is from the head. Body temperature should be about 98.4°F or 37°C.
2. Wear gloves or better still, mittens.
3. Three thin T-shirts are better than one wool sweater. The layers trap air and insulate you from cold.
4. Don't wear jeans. They give no wind protection, and are miserable when wet. Wear wool.

5. If you get wet—by falling overboard for example—keep your oilskins on, or put them on over the wet clothes. This will keep the wind out and you will warm up underneath.
6. If you get wet on the move, stay wet. Don't change into dry clothes until you stop or you'll end up with all wet clothes and nothing dry to sleep in.
7. **If you wear a cagoule or anorak, get one with a fully opening** zip, not the smock type. You can then ensure that you get adequate ventilation as the weather changes by zipping it up and down. Adjust your clothing to keep yourself pleasantly warm

So, as you can see, you might not be able to change the weather, or fight it, but if you make allowances for it, you can get along pretty well, just like the bamboo.

Chapter 10

PREPARE YOUR OWN FORECAST

WHY WORRY ABOUT WEATHER?

That's a bad question, but it's one frequently asked, or passed as comment. Why worry about the weather when you can't do anything about it.

You certainly can't change the weather, but you can prepare to combat its effects by measures, ranging from taking the right kit, to not going at all. What you must avoid doing is arriving at a mountain spot, or yacht marina, find that the weather forecast is poor, and go out regardless.

The feeling is "We've come this far to sail or climb, and, hang the weather, let's go." Having made the trip or spent the rail fare, you are going to have a bash. That's the attitude that brings the lifeboats and helicopters out.

PLAN YOUR WEATHER

You must combat impulsive behaviour in the face of bad weather, by writing a forecast for your trip, while the trip is still in the planning stages. Given common sense you will realise that bad weather is building up, and unless you are a fool, you will be half ready to act sensibly, even to the extent of not going out at all.

This does *NOT*, incidentally, mean abandoning your trip, but appreciation of the weather conditions will lead you to take the right kit, the right food, and make the right decisions.

EXPEDITION FORECASTS

In this book we have attempted to instruct a largely urban audience on the basics of weather. By now certain patterns of weather will have emerged, and you can establish a few rules for making a weather forecast of your own.

PLAN YOUR TRIP

Any outdoor enthusiast, planning a trip, makes lots of lists; lists of kit, lists of food and so on. It probably looks like this:

Trip to N. Wales

People:	—	Tom, Dick, Harry
Camp gear:	—	Tom
Climbing gear:	—	Harry
Maps:	—	Dick
Food:	—	Each, separate list
Transport:	—	Dick's car
Money:	—	How much?

etc., etc.

Let's add another heading to this list:

Weather: — All.

Make weather data one of your headings, and detail *two* people to study it separately.

Sub-headings for 'Weather' might read as follows:

Date
Length of trip (Fri. — Mon.)
Season
Temperature
Humidity
Rain
Barometer
General outlook
Local forecast
Cut out point(s)

So, under these headings, get *two* people to assemble all the data, and prepare a forecast for the whole party, of weather for this proposed weekend trip. Not what the data says, but what it *means.*

WHY TWO PEOPLE?

Let two people prepare their forecasts, and accept the worst. Always assume that, within reason, the worst forecast will be the right one. If Joe says the weather will be pretty good, and Charlie says pretty bad, believe Charlie. He may be wrong, but you are erring on the right side.

THE PRE-TRIP PLAN

Weather, as we have seen, comes in waves. What you are interested in, is establishing a weather pattern for the area in question. To do this you must have information for SEVERAL DAYS PRECEDING THE TRIP. The easiest way to assemble this information is to prepare a chart.

Information Weather Chart N. Wales Fr. Mar. 12 to Mon. 15th

	Wed. 10th	*Thurs. 11th*	*Fri. 12th*
Gen. Forecast	Poor	Improving	Fair
Local Forecast	Snow	Rain	Clear (Frost)
Temp.	—3° C	+4° C	—3° C
Pressure	988° C	995° C	1005° C
Sky	Low Stratus	Clearing	Clear
Wind	E/strong	E/falling	E/Light
Precipitation	Snow showers	Rain	Showers
T.V. Forecast	Poor	Improving	Fair
Paper	Poor	Poor/ Improving	Improving/ Fair
Local	Poor	Better	Better
Go/stay decision	Stay	Go	Go

This is a typical, indeed an actual, chart for a weekend trip hill-trekking in North Wales. The sub-headings are arbitrary, but they will, if followed, give a good idea of what you may expect on the weather front.

SOURCES OF INFORMATION

We have covered the official sources of forecasts in Chapter 2 and told you how to read them in Chapter 8. They contain all the information you will need, even for esoteric information like pressure—you get this from looking at the isobars, and noting the areas they pass through or near.

Of course, you may live in Kent and the weekend may be in North Wales. Ring your local weather centre on Wednesday, Thursday and Friday, and they will tell you what is happening, even far away up there in mountain country. Radio forecasts, being right up to date, are the most useful.

Quality newspapers like 'The Times' and 'The Guardian' (especially on Saturday) give an excellent forecast, with maps and regional reports, while the BBC gives excellent reports on radio and T.V.

LOCAL FORECASTS AND KNOWLEDGE

Let us say that you have decided to go, and eventually arrive at your starting point. Ask someone there, preferably someone likely to know, what they think the weather will do over the next few days. Local information is vital, for in the U.K. the weather is subject to much local variation.

Police Stations, mountain gear shops, or ship's chandlers (the staff usually sail or climb locally themselves and can give good advice); Lifeboat or Mountain Rescue Centre; Local Airfield; local newspaper.

Get local information and decide what to do.

ALTERNATIVE DESTINATIONS

You can, on the basis of early forecasts usually make a different trip from the one you intended, if the original one would be impossible in such weather. So always have alternative destinations in mind if the weather prevents you from moving on to the original one.

UPDATING YOUR FORECASTS

Once you are out, you probably won't get the daily papers or see much television, but you *MUST* up-date your forecasts as often as possible. Weather patterns, especially locally, can change quickly.

If you have a transistor radio, you can probably pick up weather reports—*and must note the times* and try to do so. Check that your transistor has the relevant U.K. wavelengths, as many foreign sets cannot pick up Radio 4. Try and get at least two forecasts a day. This should be the leader's responsibility. See local papers for broadcast times.

You can also ask people you meet what the latest weather forecast is; and finally, use your eyes and common sense. The more relevant information you can collect, daily, the safer you will be.

CONCLUSION

You cannot be a competent outdoor expert, or amateur, unless you can cope with the weather.

We hope this book has simplified the vast amount of weather information we can get, to the point where you can understand it, and impressed upon you the necessity of reading weather forecasts and making decisions on what they contain.

If you have done that, and you know what your weather is likely to be, then stay or go, it's your decision, and good luck to you in all your ventures.